The UNDER DOGS

FAKE IT TILL THEY MAKE IT

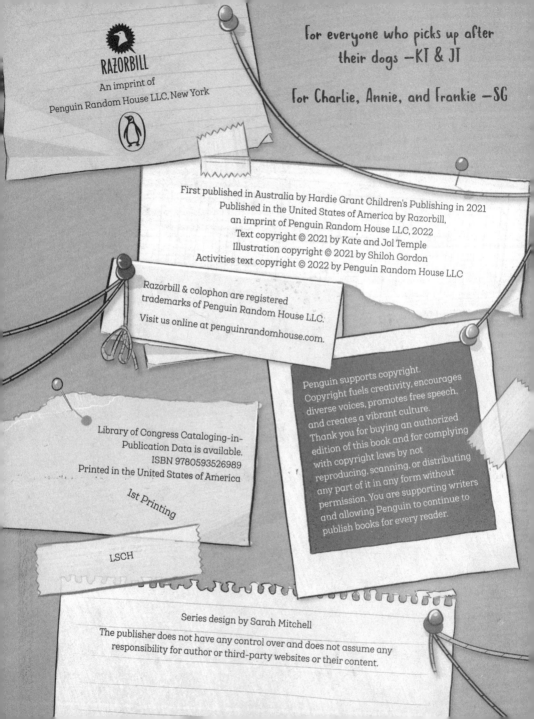

RAZORBILL

An imprint of
Penguin Random House LLC, New York

For everyone who picks up after
their dogs —KT & JT

For Charlie, Annie, and Frankie —SG

First published in Australia by Hardie Grant Children's Publishing in 2021
Published in the United States of America by Razorbill,
an imprint of Penguin Random House LLC, 2022
Text copyright © 2021 by Kate and Jol Temple
Illustration copyright © 2021 by Shiloh Gordon
Activities text copyright © 2022 by Penguin Random House LLC

Razorbill & colophon are registered
trademarks of Penguin Random House LLC.

Visit us online at penguinrandomhouse.com.

Library of Congress Cataloging-in-
Publication Data is available.
ISBN 9780593526989
Printed in the United States of America

1st Printing

LSCH

Series design by Sarah Mitchell

The publisher does not have any control over and does not assume any
responsibility for author or third-party websites or their content.

KATE AND JOL TEMPLE

The UNDER DOGS

FAKE IT TILL THEY MAKE IT

ART BY
SHILOH
GORDON

RAZORBILL

CHAPTER 1

Have you ever been to a detective agency?
A **real** detective agency? With **REAL** detectives?

Me neither.

And neither had the **Underdogs**. This is them here.

Barkley is a German shepherd, and sort of the boss.

This is **Dr. Spots**. She's a Dalmatian and an inventor.

You might be wondering why a bunch of underdog detectives are playing **ping-pong** instead of **cracking cases**.

Well, that's because Dogtown already has **proper** detectives.

They're called the **Top Dogs**. This is them on the billboard.

Why'd they have to put that billboard on top of **OUR** office?

TOP DOGS IN DOGTOWN

The Top Dogs are **really** famous. They even have their own reality TV show (and it's pretty good, too).

So if you need a **detective** in Dogtown, **that's** who you call. Not the Underdogs.

Yes, things had sure been quiet for the Underdogs.

Barkley took a look around their **shabby** office, with its **peeling** paint and **broken** furniture.

If they could just get a few more **customers**, maybe they could **jazz** this place up a little.

Or they could move to a **nicer** office that wasn't upstairs from a soup factory!

Barkley sighed, and as he did, the smell of soup hit his wet nose. Turnip and cabbage. **YUCK!**

But a **fancy** office with no soup stench would cost a lot of money.

The Underdogs needed to start solving cases, and **fast**!

Last week Barkley thought they had a case, but it turned out to be a **delivery dog** with a crate of broccoli for the soup factory.

Anyone order 20 boxes of broccoli?

With no cases to solve, the Underdogs were keeping **busy** in other ways.

Dr. Spots was inventing a **tennis ball** that came back to you so you didn't have to chase it.

Fang was learning how to **tie knots**.

Carl had taken up **oil painting**.

And Barkley was practicing his **golf putting**.

Just then, the phone rang.

"**AAAAAGH!** The phone is broken! Why is it doing that? **AHHHHHH!**"

Barkley shook his head. "It's a **phone**, Carl. It's called '**ringing**.' How many times do I have to tell you that?"

"Oh. Right. Ringing … yes, I **remember**. Should I pick it up?" asked Carl, looking unsure.

"Hello, this is Carl. Nice to meet you," said Carl.

Barkley **snatched** the phone. "Gimme that!" he grumbled. "Hello, this is the Underdog Detective Agency. No clue left undug."

It **wasn't** a case. It was a **pizza order**.

"You want a what? A pepperoni? On a gluten-free base? I think you've got the **wrong** number," snapped Barkley.

But Carl wasted no time. In an instant, he was **flinging** pizza dough in the air in the Underdogs' kitchenette. "Coming right up!" he said.

"We're **not** a pizza shop! We're a detective agency," barked Barkley. He was just about to say something else when there was a **knock** at the door.

KNOCK!
KNOCK!

10

"**AAAAAGH!** Why is the door making that noise?!"
shrieked Carl.

"It'll just be someone looking for the **soup factory**,"
sighed Fang.

The door swung open.

"The soup factory is **downstairs**–" Fang started to say,
then stopped.

At the door stood a **dog**. Not just **any** dog–a very

important dog. A very **FAMOUS** dog...

He **wasn't** looking for the soup factory.
He **didn't** have a delivery of broccoli or turnips.

He had a **case** that needed **solving**, and he was
looking for the only detectives that could help him.

Are you the
Underdogs?

CHAPTER 2

Carl let out an excited yelp, "**PUPLO PICASSO!**"

Sure enough, it was none other than the world-famous **artist** Puplo Picasso.

He wore a **beret**, and his tail was covered in **spots** of colored paint.

Carl was a **BIG** fan.

PUPLO!

Wow!

Impressive!

Barkley, on the other paw, had **never** heard of him. "Hello. How can I help you?" he asked.

"I'm Puplo Picasso. The **famous** painter. You've heard of me, of course," said Puplo.

Of course they'd heard of him— **everyone** had heard of him!

Except Barkley...

PUPLO PICASSO:
- World-famous artist (and knows it!)
- Wears a beret
- Tail often covered in paint splotches

Barkley looked Puplo up and down. He was **confused**. Sure, their office needed a coat of paint, but he didn't remember calling a **painter**. "Well, thanks for dropping by. But we'll need to solve a few more cases before we get around to painting the place …"

Puplo snorted. "I'm not **THAT** kind of painter."

"Barkley, this dog is the most famous artist in the world! His paintings sell for **millions**!" cried Carl.

"It's true," replied Puplo. "My paintings are the **best** in the world. And that's exactly why I'm here—I **need** your help."

Barkley took a second look. Nope, he still didn't **recognize** him. "OK, Puplo, what is it we can do for you today?" he asked.

Puplo **slumped** down on a wobbly chair and put his head in his paws. "One of my **masterpieces** has gone **missing** from the Dogtown Art Gallery!" he cried. "And it's supposed to go on display **tonight** at a big gallery opening. Everyone will be there!"

"Ooh, can we come?" asked Carl.

PLEASE! PLEASE!

"You **MUST** come," said Puplo. "I need you there to solve the case of my missing masterpiece!"

"Well, you know the Underdog Detectives are the **best** in the business. No clue left **undug**. I'm glad you came to us first," said Barkley.

Actually, I tried the Top Dogs first, but they're out of town. I called their office and was told they're on a skiing trip up in Dog Whistler and won't be back until Thursday. I can't wait that long—I'm **DESPERATE** to solve this mystery now!

Barkley and Fang looked at each other. Thursday was only **two** days away!

They'd need to **solve** this case in just two days… before the Top Dogs got back.

It wasn't much time, but the Underdogs **needed** this case, and they weren't about to let it get away.

"Lucky for you, the boss of the Dogtown Art Gallery **insisted** I ask the Underdogs. I'd never even heard of you. So here I am, but as soon as the **Top Dogs** get back, I'm giving them the case," said Puplo.

"Unless we solve it **first**," said Fang.

"Precisely," said Puplo.

"A missing masterpiece..." said Barkley. "This is a very interesting case. Can you **describe** the painting?"

Puplo sighed. "**IMPOSSIBLE!** My art speaks for itself."

"Just a minute, Mr. Picasso," said Fang. "Art doesn't **talk**. Dogs talk. Cats talk. Plus goldfish, lemurs, and most birds... but a **painting** can't talk. Am I right, Spots?"

Dr. Spots looked up from where she was **tinkering** with her latest invention.

Correct, Fang. Technically paintings can't talk for themselves. Even if you were to draw a big mouth, it wouldn't have the vocal cords required for speech.

"So a painting can't **actually** talk … interesting," mused Carl.

Puplo **shook** his head and made a move for the door. Maybe this wasn't such a good idea. "I knew I should have **waited** for the Top Dogs," he said.

I'll see myself out.

But Barkley **jumped** to his feet.

Now wait a minute, Mr. Picasso. Any case that the Top Dogs can solve, we can solve faster. Right, Underdogs?

I wouldn't have thought so . . .

Puplo looked at the Underdogs. What a **ragtag** bunch of dogs!

But what choice did he have? They were the **only** detectives in town... at least for two days.

So he decided to give them a **shot**. What's the worst that could happen?

"Fine. You have until **Thursday**. If the case isn't solved by then, I'm giving it to the Top Dogs."

Deal!

Fang's ears pricked up. She'd had an **idea**. A light bulb went off (not an **actual** light bulb, because they hadn't paid the electricity bill).

"Hang on, Puplo. One question. Wouldn't we have heard if a **famous** painting went missing from the Dogtown Art Gallery? That would be **front-page news**!"

Puplo smiled.

You're pretty smart for a cat. Meet me at the gallery in one hour, and I'll explain everything.

CHAPTER 3

Fang couldn't believe it. A painting worth **millions** had gone missing, and it was their job to solve the mystery. What a **great** case!

It didn't get better than this. This was what being a **REAL** detective was all about.

Besides, Fang **liked** trips to the art gallery. Barkley, on the other paw, wasn't so sure. He'd **never** set foot in an art gallery.

This is going to be great!

Still, a case was a case, so Barkley and Fang wasted no time jumping on the detective **bicycle** … Well, they wasted a little bit of time, because the tandem bicycle was missing a **seat**!

So Fang jumped on an old **scooter** that made a **clanking** noise, and Barkley took the bike.

Pretty soon after that, they were **hightailing** it to the art gallery.

They **zipped** through Dogtown Central Park with the wind in their fur.

They passed **cafés** with dogs sipping **puppychinos** and **bone broth**.

They **sped** around **office blocks** where dogs worked like dogs...

and finally they arrived at the art gallery.

It was a **fancy** old building with tall marble columns and wide steps.

Fang **smiled**. Barkley **shivered**.

The two detectives parked the scooter and the bike and walked into the art gallery.

"What's wrong?" asked Fang.

"Art galleries! They give me the **creeps**," replied Barkley.

"Whaaat? Art galleries are *FUN!*"

"Not to me they're not. All those paintings of dogs staring at me give me the **heebie-jeebies**," said Barkley.

I'm not sure about this place, Fang . . .

"It'll be fine!" said Fang. "When I was a kitten, my parents always took me to the art gallery, and I **loved** it. And now we're here working on a **case** with a famous artist as well. This is the **best**!"

The pair walked into a room filled with **weird** sculptures.

GO FETCH
DOGATELLO

MODERN ART

LOBSTER PHONE
SALVADOG DALI

Barkley didn't know **what** to think of it, but he knew Fang was right.

"If we're going to solve this case, we're going to need to know **everything** there is to know about art. But before we go any further, I just need to use the **toilet**. Excuse me," said Barkley.

Barkley was just about to lift his **leg** on a conveniently placed fire hydrant, when...

"**STOPPPPPPP!**" yelled a security guard. He was a tall, curly-looking groodle who had a walkie-talkie in one hand and an **angry** expression on his face.

DO NOT WHIZ ON THE ART!

"That's **art**? It looks like a **toilet**!" said Barkley.

"It's art. Read the sign!"

"Oh, sorry," said Barkley, feeling embarrassed. "And I suppose that **tin** of **sardines** is art, too?"

"Don't **EAT** the art!" barked the security guard. "I've got my eye on you two!"

Barkley and Fang **scurried** off into the next room looking for Puplo, with Fang wiping the sardines off her **whiskers**. "Friendly fellow," she said.

"I told you I **hate** art galleries," said Barkley. "Now, where's our famous artist?"

The detectives wandered around the art gallery until they came to a **very fancy** room with a **round** roof and **arched** doorway.

WOW!

"This looks like the place," said Barkley.

The room was full of workers hanging paintings, getting everything ready for the **big opening**.

And there, in the middle of the room, sat Puplo Picasso. In front of him was a **large** painting.

"Ah! Underdogs! So glad you're here. Now you can **solve** the **case** of my missing masterpiece. This is the missing painting." Puplo pointed a paw at the **large** painting on the wall.

Barkley scratched his head. "But, Puplo, the painting is right **there**! How can it be missing?" he said.

This wasn't making **sense** at all.

"It's a **FAKE!**" cried Puplo. "This is **not** my painting. It's
a very good **imitation**, but I didn't paint it. Look, you
can see right down here..." Puplo pointed to a paw
print in the corner. "That's not my **paw print**. Someone
switched my painting!"

CHAPTER 4

"Someone **switched** the painting?" asked Fang.
Puplo nodded furiously.

"Hmm…" said Barkley. "How **strange**. Surely someone
would notice if the painting was swapped…"

"No one noticed! Not until I did," said Puplo. "You see,
I have a **brilliant** eye!"

"I guess your eyes are quite **nice**…" said Barkley
awkwardly.

"So, you **didn't** paint this?" asked Fang suspiciously. This didn't add up. How could a masterpiece just go missing without **anyone** noticing?

Fang was beginning to feel like someone was pulling her tail.

Actually, someone **was** pulling her tail.

Fang spun around. There stood a snooty-looking **corgi** with a shiny coat, little spectacles, and a bow tie.

"Greetings, Top Dogs," said the corgi, **nervously** shaking Fang's tail.

So glad you're here!

The corgi looked at the **tail**. He looked at Fang. "Wait, you're not the Top Dogs…"

"No, we're not the Top Dogs. We're the Underdogs," said Barkley.

"Oh! Thank goodness," exclaimed the corgi.

Barkley was pleasantly **surprised**. It wasn't too often that people actually wanted the Underdogs and **NOT** the Top Dogs.

Fang took her tail back and **stuck** out a **paw**.
"Underdogs at your service."

"But you're a **cat**." The corgi frowned. "How odd ..."

"Right again," said Fang. "And **who** exactly are you?"

I am Sir Basil Dogbone, the manager of this fine and magnificent gallery. It was I who suggested Puplo call **YOU**, but he insisted on the Top Dogs.

SIR BASIL DOGBONE:
- A snack-loving corgi
- Manager of the Dogtown Art Gallery
- Art expert

"The Top Dogs are the **best**!" said Puplo.

"I'm sure the Underdogs will do a **stellar** job!" said Sir Basil. "You see, I've heard about your reputation, and I just knew you could help us get our precious masterpiece back."

Barkley was **flattered**. Finally, word was getting out about the Underdogs!

If they cracked this case, they'd be back on **top**.

But right now, Barkley needed to find out what this Sir Basil Dogbone knew about the **missing** painting.

"So, you're in charge of this gallery?" asked Barkley.

"Correct," replied Sir Basil Dogbone.

"That means you must know **all** the paintings here?"

"Like the **back** of my **paw**," said Sir Basil.

Then wouldn't you have noticed that Puplo's masterpiece was swapped for this fake?

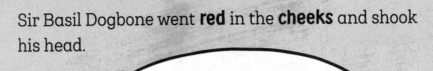

Sir Basil Dogbone went **red** in the **cheeks** and shook his head.

I'm embarrassed to say I had no idea! Not until Puplo pointed it out. You see, this fake is so good it even tricked me.

I'm ashamed! But it's really a magnificent fake—the artist who painted it must be very talented. You could say it's a **PAWFECT** imitation.

The only difference is the real one is worth millions!

They didn't have a high-tech lab, but it sure sounded good.

"IMPOSSIBLE!" barked Sir Basil. "Puplo's exhibition is tonight! This painting must stay—we don't want word getting out that the **real** one has gone **missing**!"

Barkley thought about that for a moment. Maybe there was **another** way.

"OK," agreed Barkley. "But we'll need to send Dr. Spots down here to take a **look** at it."

Sir Basil Dogbone wasn't so sure. He scratched his head.

"I don't know…" he mumbled. "I wouldn't want to bother your **chief scientist**."

"I insist the painting be **examined**!" snorted Puplo.

Sir Basil nodded in agreement. "Well, OK. But Dr. Spots will need to be quick. Your opening is only **hours** away!"

"We can be fast. We have an **electric sports car** with **turbo boosters**," said Fang.

"No, we don't . . ." said Barkley.

"OK, we don't. But we do have a **bicycle**." Fang didn't mention the missing seat. "Dr. Spots can be here before the exhibition opens."

Sir Basil Dogbone and Puplo agreed, so Barkley and Fang said goodbye and **hurried** towards the exit.

They needed to call Dr. Spots and get her down to the gallery–and **fast**.

On the way out, Barkley couldn't help but notice some of the art. It wasn't **half bad**, really. Maybe he could get the hang of this art stuff after all.

He stopped right in front of a **sculpture**. "Pretty interesting …" he said admiringly.

Fang sighed. "Barkley, that's the **toilet door**."

"Oh. I thought it was **art**!" said Barkley.

Fang shook her head, but just as she did, **something** caught her eye.

One thing about cats is that they can see out of the corners of their eyes...and that's **exactly** what happened here.

Standing by one of the paintings was a small character in a black **coat** and **hat**. He looked very familiar.

"Hey, Barkley...isn't that...?" said Fang.

Barkley spun around, his ears pricking up. "**RATZAK!** The **sneakiest** rat in town...what's he doing here?"

Just at that moment, Ratzak noticed the Underdogs. He pulled his hat over his face, but it was **too late**. The Underdogs had seen him.

As quick as a **flash**, Ratzak hit the floor and scurried out of the gallery.

"We'll text Dr. Spots from the road, Fang," said Barkley, making a **quick** exit. "Right now, we have to **FOLLOW THAT RAT!**"

GET BACK HERE, RATZAK!

CHAPTER 5

Back out on the street, Ratzak made a **sneaky** turn.

He was **quick**, he was **sharp**, and he knew every alley and back lane in Dogtown. He wasn't going to be easy to follow.

Barkley stopped next to his bike. Now it was missing **two** seats!

WHY DOES THIS KEEP HAPPENING?!

You'll have to ride with me!

Fang and Barkley darted down the busy street, **dodging** dogs on the **clanky** old scooter.

Ratzak was trying to lose them in the **crowd**, but the Underdogs didn't take their eyes off him.

Even the **sweet** smell of donuts from a street vendor didn't distract them.

They went over a **speed bump** that made the scooter **rattle** and **clang**.

Ratzak turned to see where the noise was coming from and caught their **reflection** in a McDoggles restaurant.

AHH!

Now Ratzak was **running**. Running **FAST!**

Ratzak **zipped** down a narrow back lane and popped up on the fancy street where all the **fashionable** dogs shopped.

Fang and Barkley clanged their rusty old scooter down the street, **swerving** past the fancy dogs, but Ratzak jumped on a passing streetcar and **disappeared** from view.

The Underdogs had **lost** him.

"Drat!" said Fang.

"Don't worry," said Barkley. "We know where he lives... let's just meet him at **home**."

While Barkley and Fang were making their way to Ratzak's nest, Dr. Spots and Carl were already at the **gallery**.

Dr. Spots quickly got to work **examining** the painting.

And Carl got to work on an art project...

"Crumbs!" said Dr. Spots, peering at the **canvas** under the **microscope**. Puplo and Sir Basil gathered around.

"What is it?" asked Puplo, eager for any information that would help **crack** the case.

"It's **crumbs**. Dog food crumbs. Look."

Puplo took a look through the microscope.

Sure enough, he could see little crumbs **stuck** in the paint. The kind you find right at the bottom of a packet of **dog food**.

"Whoever painted this was having a yummy, yummy **snack** at the time," said Dr. Spots.

Puplo took a closer look. "Disgusting! I **NEVER** eat when I'm painting!"

"I'm going to need to run some **tests** on these," said Dr. Spots, **scraping** the crumbs off the painting and into a little bag.

"What else can you tell us about this **fake** artwork?" asked Sir Basil.

Dr. Spots beamed. "Well, it's lovely, don't you think? Great **colors**, nice **linework**, good **composition**…"

"I agree," said Sir Basil, "but can you tell it's a fake?"

"Naturally. Look at this **paw print** compared to Puplo's. Slightly smaller. Shorter claws. There's no way this is Puplo's signature."

It was a good **imitation** all right, but not good enough to fool Puplo or Dr. Spots.

60

"It's a very good fake. Even the canvas is **identical** to a genuine Puplo Picasso. This is the work of a real **master**!" said Dr. Spots.

"So is this!" said Carl, holding up one of his sculptures— a can of **soup** with some **paper clips** sticking out of it.

It was not very good, but Puplo smiled. "Very good, Carl. You're very **talented**. Maybe one day your work might be on display in this gallery, too."

Carl's eyes lit up. "You think so?"

"No," said Puplo.

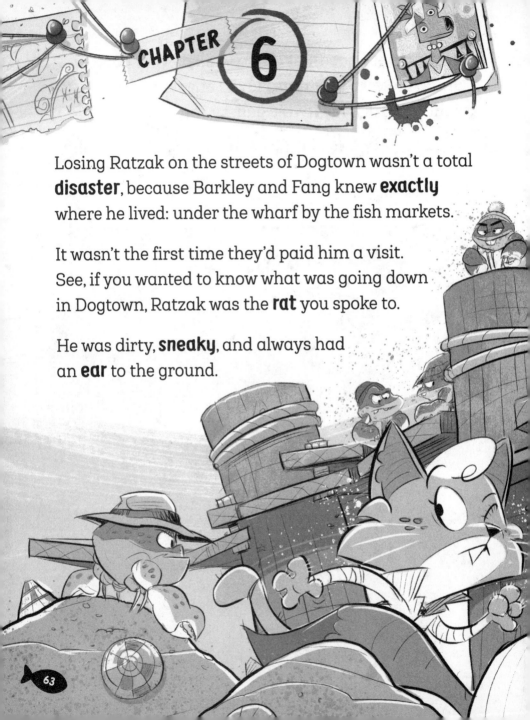

CHAPTER 6

Losing Ratzak on the streets of Dogtown wasn't a total **disaster**, because Barkley and Fang knew **exactly** where he lived: under the wharf by the fish markets.

It wasn't the first time they'd paid him a visit. See, if you wanted to know what was going down in Dogtown, Ratzak was the **rat** you spoke to.

He was dirty, **sneaky**, and always had an **ear** to the ground.

But **what** was Ratzak doing at the art gallery?
And **why** was he running away from them?

It was all very **suspicious**.

Barkley and Fang ducked under the wharf and **crawled**
along until they reached a small door with a sign that
said **DO NOT DISTURB**.

Barkley ignored it and knocked **loudly**.

A **small** voice came from the other side of the door. "There's nobody home."

Barkley knew that voice **anywhere**. "Open up, Ratzak," he barked.

"Who is it?" replied Ratzak.

"It's the Underdogs," said Fang. "The **best** detectives in town."

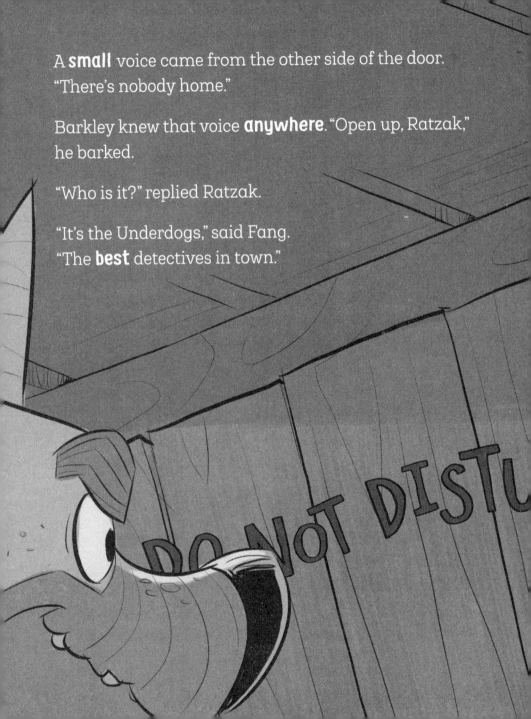

The door **creaked** open.

"Ha ha! That's funny," sneered Ratzak through the **crack** in the door.

"We need to talk to you," said Fang. "Won't take long."

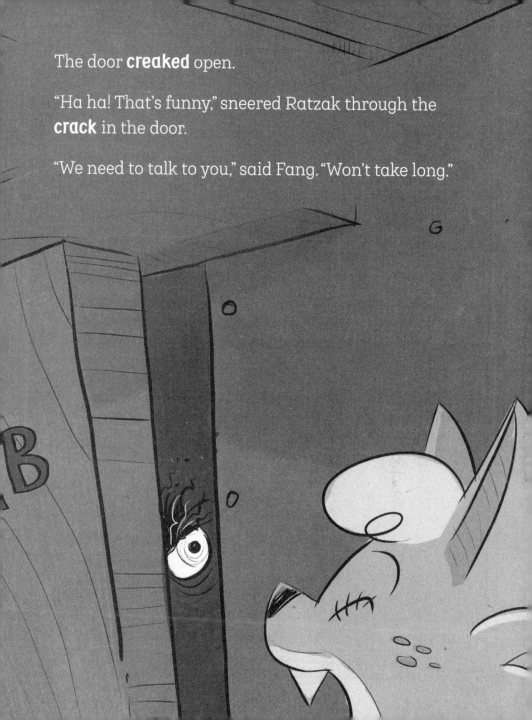

Ratzak looked Fang up and down, and let out a little **shiver**. He wasn't a **fan** of cats.

"Cats never just want to **talk**…"

"We'll make it worth your while. How does two **cheese slices** sound?" added Barkley.

In this line of business, Barkley knew a cheese slice could come in **handy**.

Ratzak sniffed the air. The smell of those two cheese slices was too **delightful** to resist.

"OK … fine. Come in," grumbled Ratzak, **snatching** up the cheese.

Fang and Barkley shuffled inside the rat's **nest**…
except it **wasn't** such a rat's nest after all.

Ratzak had done the place up since the Underdogs
were last there. There was a nice lamp in the corner,
a rug, some **snazzy-looking** furniture, and… some
very nice paintings!

"**WOW!**" said Fang. "I like what you've done to the place, Ratzak. Very fancy."

And very *suspicious*, thought Fang.

Ratzak **gobbled** up the two cheese slices immediately. "So, what can I do for the famous Blunderdogs?"

"Why don't you tell us what you were doing at the art gallery today?" asked Barkley.

"The **art gallery**?" asked Ratzak.

"Yeah. It's a big building **downtown** with lots of art in it," snapped Fang.

"Never heard of it," lied Ratzak.

Fang **HISSED**.

Ratzak **gulped**.

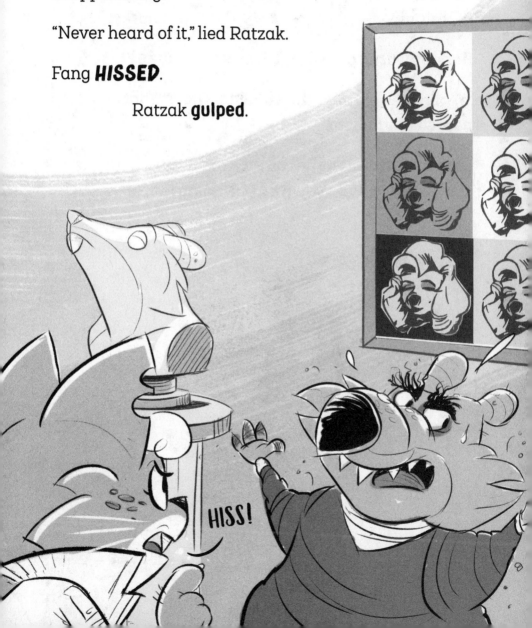

HISS!

"OK, OK. I know the art gallery. Let me see … what was I doing? Oh yeah. I think I popped in by **mistake**. Yeah, that's right—I thought it was … the supermarket."

Barkley wasn't convinced. "The **supermarket**?"

"Yeah, I was all out of **toothpaste**. That's what it was! I needed toothpaste!"

Barkley growled at the rodent. "You're not fooling us, Ratzak. What were you **REALLY** doing there?"

The rat **wailed**. "OK, OK! But if I tell you, you've got to **promise** not to tell anybody else."

Barkley nodded.

"… I **really** like art," said the embarrassed rat.

Fang and Barkley looked at each other, then back at Ratzak.

"I know what you're thinking … us rats don't like the **finer** things in life. Well, you're **WRONG!** Why can't a rat enjoy looking at a masterpiece? Why can't a rat have a nice lamp or a few pictures on the wall? What's so **wrong** with that?"

Fang wasn't sure. It sounded too **strange** to be true. "Something smells **fishy**," she said.

"You **are** right next to the fish market, what did you expect?" sneered the rat.

"So where did you get all these **great** paintings from?" asked Fang, looking around.

"Must have cost a lot of money," added Barkley.

"Actually, for your bone-brain information... they didn't cost **ANYTHING**. I painted them."

"**YOU!**" said Fang and Barkley together.

"Oh, this **street rat** isn't good enough to make art?!" snapped Ratzak. "You sound just like my **four hundred** brothers and sisters. They think I'm getting too big for my boots, but I've got just as much right to make art as anyone else. I'm not a **fake**."

Fang and Barkley thought about it for a second... or three. If Ratzak was telling the truth, he had a point. Anyone can **like** art. Anyone can **make** art...

But Ratzak?

"Just because you like making art **doesn't** make you a fake, Ratzak," said Barkley. "But a fake is the **reason** we're here. Somebody **swapped** a real Puplo Picasso painting for a fake one at the gallery. What do you know about that?"

Ratzak shrugged. "It wasn't me!"

Fang wasn't so sure. If Ratzak had painted all the art in his house, maybe **HE** was the faker.

I swear it wasn't me!

But Barkley had another idea. "Maybe it was an **inside job**," he mused.

"Well, yes, the artwork was inside…" said Fang.

"No, dummy, he means the thief must work **INSIDE** the gallery," sniggered Ratzak. "Only somebody with access to the painting could have pulled off a **stunt** like that."

Fang thought about it. It made sense. It would be **impossible** to get a painting that big out of the gallery without being noticed by…

THE SECURITY GUARD!

"That **barky** groodle?" asked Barkley.

"Yeah, I know him," said Ratzak. "He did some time in the pound for **stealing** bones back in the day. What's his name again? Some kind of **car** part?"

Headlight?

Hubcap??

That's it! **AXEL!**

AXEL:
- Groodle security guard
- Loves napping on the job
- Dislikes cheese

Back on their **clunky** old scooter, Barkley called the agency. He wanted to see what **clues** Dr. Spots had found at the gallery.

Carl answered the phone. "Hello, Underdogs here. Can I take your **pizza** order?"

"Carl, it's me!"

"Hi, Barkley! Would you like a side order of garlic bread with your pizza?"

"Put Spots on the phone!" said Barkley.

"Barkley, I found crumbs in the fake painting. I'm running some tests, but I need more time to work out what they are."

"Great work, Spots. While you keep investigating, Fang and I will go to Puplo's art opening. The faker could be there."

"Carl will meet you there with your disguises. You better hurry! The art opening starts in ten minutes."

Ten minutes might be enough time to get back to the gallery in a **chopper** or a **jet pack**, but on a rusty old **scooter**, it was almost impossible.

Luckily, Barkley knew Dogtown like the back of his paw.

He and Fang **zipped** and **zagged** through the streets, taking all the shortcuts and skipping all the longcuts.

Finally, they came to a **screeching** halt back outside the gallery.

Fang and Barkley looked for Carl, but all they could see was a **bowl of fruit** calling their names.

FANG!
BARKLEY!

"Psst!" said the **fruit bowl**. "It's me, Carl."

"Nice disguise, Carl. I thought you were a fruit bowl," said Fang.

"I am," said Carl. "Here are your **disguises**. I made them myself. No one will suspect you!" Carl handed over a bag and looked around **carefully**. No one had seen them.

"We'll get changed and see you in there," said Fang. "Barkley, keep an eye out for that security guard."

Once they got **inside**, it didn't take long for Fang and Barkley to find Axel.

The security guard was sitting at the entrance with his eyes half closed. He **sniffed** the air as the two Underdogs strolled over…

After making a **face**, the security guard yawned and pulled his hat over his eyes.

"He doesn't look like much of an **art faker**. He looks half asleep!" said Fang.

"That might be **exactly** what he wants us to think," said Barkley. Fang nodded, and the pair entered the **party**.

The room was full of **arty** dogs. Sir Basil was among them, showing off the gallery's newest paintings.

But what caught Fang's eye wasn't the fancy dogs.

It was a very familiar and very **fishy** figure in a dark coat, who was **sneaking** past the sleeping security guard and making a beeline for one of the big **masterpieces**.

"Look who's back," said Fang, **pointing** across the room.

Barkley looked up.

RATZAK.

"Seems he just can't stay away. And look—he's got a new **nose**," said Barkley.

He was right. Ratzak was in **disguise**.

Fang and Barkley **sidled** up to Ratzak. "We have to stop bumping into each other like this," said Barkley.

Ratzak **gasped**, then frowned. "Oh, it's just you. I thought you were a giant talking can of cheese soup."

"What are you doing here, Ratzak?" asked Fang.

"How many **times** have I gotta tell you?" sighed the rat. "I like the art."

Fang wasn't convinced.

Why the fake nose? Why the sneaking? If you just like art, why do you need the disguise?

Ratzak **sneered**. "You're dressed like a soup can, and you're picking on my **nose**?"

"I never pick noses," protested Fang.

"You Underdogs think you're so **clever**, but you don't get it," hissed Ratzak. "Who's going to let a rat into an art gallery?"

At that moment, they were interrupted by a waiter carrying a large tray of **Woof-O-Bites**.

"Snacks?" asked the waiter.

"No thanks. I just came for the art," grumbled Ratzak, and he **disappeared** off into the crowd.

Ratzak might not have been a fan of **doggy treats**, but Barkley sure was. He took a **big** pawful and gobbled them up. "Mmmm, my favorite! Cheesy Woof-O-Bites."

Sir Basil came over to say hello, **snapping** up some Woof-O-Bites. "Yes indeed. I arranged the catering myself—nothing but the **best** for the art lovers of Dogtown. I'm Sir Basil Dogbone. And you are…?"

It's us. Fang and Barkley. We're in disguise.

91

"Ah, yes! The Underdogs. Wonderful to see you here."
Basil leaned in. "Are you any closer to **solving** the case?"

"You could say we've got our **eyes** on a suspect," Barkley
said, looking across the room to where Axel the security
dog was snoring.

"Excellent! Now, let me introduce you to one of
Dogtown's **newest** artists." Sir Basil ushered them
through the crowd towards a **familiar-looking**
Chihuahua.

CHAPTER 8

"Underdogs, have you met Carl?"

"CARL!"

"Yes, he's a real **talent**. Look at his latest work."

Carl was standing in front of a painting.
It was of a **soup can**.

Hey, guys!
I got inspired by
the soup factory!

SOUP

"I see a very **bright** future for this pup." Sir Basil smiled.

Just then, Puplo joined them. His face was **white**. Well, it was always white—but this time it was even whiter.

"Disaster! Another painting is gone!" gasped Puplo.

"You mean there's another **FAKE?**" asked Fang.

The artist **pushed** through the crowd to where a painting should have been hanging on the wall. There was **nothing** but a **blank** space.

"Look! Another of my paintings **stolen!** You Underdogs better find it, or I'll call someone who can—the Top Dogs!"

Sir Basil **gasped**.

Barkley **scanned** the room. There were people everywhere, but **one** person was noticeably missing. The security guard. He was gone, and his empty chair was **spinning**.

"Come on, Fang!" yelped Barkley. "There's no time to waste!"

Fang and Barkley **raced** out of the party and down the hallway. It was time to **catch** their **crook**.

But **where** could he be? The hallway was long and had lots of doors. Barkley and Fang weren't sure where to start.

Fang pointed to a door with **Security Office** written on it. "Maybe in there?" she suggested.

They entered without knocking. There was **nobody** inside.

The room was full of TVs showing security **footage** of every room in the **entire** art gallery.

Fang looked around. But there wasn't much to go on. The desk was pretty **neat**—not even an old puppychino mug. All they found was a **notepad** with a few scribbles in it.

Barkley scratched his head. (It was probably **fleas**.)

"Remember what Ratzak said about Axel? How he spent time in the pound for **stealing** bones? Well, they do say a **leopard** never changes its **spots**..." said Barkley.

"Do you think the thief is a leopard? I'll call headquarters and ask Spots to run a **background check** on all the leopards in Dogtown."

It's just a saying, Fang. It means that people never really change their ways. But I'm not so sure . . . there's nothing here.

Fang scratched her soup-can hat. "He **has** to be the art thief. But if the paintings aren't here, where else would he **hide** them?"

At that moment, Sir Basil **burst** in.

Puplo was right behind him.

Sir Basil **grabbed** the artist by the **shoulders**.
"Good news, Puplo! We know who did it.
It's the **security guard**!"

Puplo gasped.

GASP!

"Yes," added Sir Basil, "the Underdogs are doing a
wonderful job, Puplo. Maybe if we just help them
look for clues, we can **solve** this right now…"
He **rummaged** through the security office.

"**OH MY DOG!** Look!"

Sir Basil had **flipped** around the security bulletin board. There, stuck on the back of it, was Puplo's **second** missing masterpiece.

Barkley took a good look. "Looks like this leopard hasn't changed his spots after all."

"But Axel is a **groodle**, not a leopard …?" said Sir Basil, looking confused.

Before Fang could explain this saying, which she'd only just heard herself, Barkley's phone **buzzed** with a new **message** from Dr. Spots.

It said three-and-a-half very **important** words:

CHEESY
WOOF
-O-
BITES!

CHAPTER 9

"Woof-O-Bites?" said Barkley.

"Woof-O-Bites!" agreed Sir Basil. "Indeed, this calls for a **celebration**."

Barkley frowned. They may have found **one** painting, but one of the artworks was **still** missing. "I'm glad you're happy, Sir Basil, but we've got work to do. The **culprit** is still at large."

Fang looked confused.

"At **large**? I thought Axel was more of a medium-sized dog..."

It's a detective saying, Fang. It means that the crook is still out there.

"Oh, I see," said Fang. "Well, we should keep looking for him!"

Barkley looked at the security TVs showing a view of every **inch** of the gallery. "I think this might be the best place to find him. Why don't we **wait** right here?"

"Wonderful idea. Yes, you stay here. I'm sure he'll turn up," said Sir Basil.

So Puplo and Sir Basil returned to the **party**, while Fang and Barkley made themselves at home in the **security** room.

Barkley and Fang **watched** and **waited**...

and **waited**...

and **waited**...

107

and **waited**.

Nothing happened.
No sign of Axel.

Sooooooo bored right now!

Barkley nodded. "This is taking too long. We need to find some clues—and **fast**."

"We don't want the Top Dogs taking over," said Fang.

Barkley jumped to his feet. "Definitely not! That's it—it's time for some good old-fashioned **detective** work. Let's get back out there and see what clues we can **sniff** out."

Fang had an idea.

"What if we **measure** the fake paw print and see if we can match it to Axel, or to any of the other **guests** while we're at it?"

"Now you're thinking like a **detective**. Let's do it."

It's time to set the soup among the pigeons!

What does that even mean?

But Fang didn't answer—she was already out the door.

The crowd had grown even **more**.

Lots of **dogs**, a few **cats**, a couple of **lemurs**, the occasional **bird**—art lovers of all kinds mooched around the room admiring the paintings and eating Woof-O-Bites.

You take this side of the room, I'll take the other.

Fang and Barkley began **sneaking** through the crowd, **measuring** paws and trying not to be noticed…

At one point, Fang stood so still that someone put their **drink** on her head.

HEY!

But none of them were an **exact** match...

They needed to find Axel, their main **suspect**, so they could measure his **paw**—but he was nowhere to be seen.

Then Barkley had a **hunch** ... a hunch that he needed to pee.

But there was someone in the toilet, so he waited. The more he waited, the more he **REALLY NEEDED TO PEE!**

He waited some more. And then he **REALLY, REALLY NEEDED TO PEE!**

"Come on!" yelped Barkley. "I can't **wait** anymore!"

Barkley tried the handle. **LOCKED!**

If Barkley had to wait any longer, something **terrible** was going to happen. With a running **leap**, he heaved his shoulder into the door.

BANG! It opened.

Standing in the bathroom was Axel. Eating a **bone**.
GROSS!

He looked surprised to see Barkley.

Barkley was just as surprised. "Axel! What are you doing in here! And why are you eating a bone in the **toilet**?!"

"Someone **locked** me in here!" growled Axel. "I thought I'd have a snack while I waited for someone to let me out. So, thanks…"

117

"Not so fast," snapped Barkley. "How did you get locked in a toilet? Are you sure you weren't **hiding** from us?"

Hiding! From you Blunderdogs? Not a chance. Sir Basil asked me to check the toilets, and the next thing I knew, someone had locked me in.

"A **likely** story," snorted Barkley. "Stop **messing** around. Where are the two missing paintings?"

Axel looked surprised. "What are you talking about? I think I would know if a **second** painting was missing. I **AM** head of security."

Fang **raced** over, almost tripping over her hat.

"Barkley, Axel is **not** our art thief," she panted.

"Of course he's the art thief. We found the second stolen painting in his office!" said Barkley.

Fang nodded. It was true. They **HAD** found the painting in Axel's office.

But there was **more** to this case than meets the eye.

Fang stuck her hand in her **pocket** and held out a packet of Woof-O-Bites.

"Care for a Woof-O-Bite, Axel?" said Fang. "They're **cheese** flavored."

"Cheese? No thank you." Axel **screwed** up his nose. "I can't stand the stuff. Besides, I'm more of a **bone** kind of dog."

CHAPTER 10

Barkley's eyes **flashed**. He sure had made the right move hiring this cat to be a dog detective. Fang was **smart** and she was **quick**–a true Underdog.

"So you don't think Axel is the art **faker**?" asked Barkley.

"I **know** he's not," said Fang. "He doesn't like cheese, and these Woof-O-Bites are **cheese** flavored..."

"**YUCK!**" gagged Axel. "Even the word 'cheese' makes me **sick**."

And look at his paws. They're so big and stubby!

"Hey!" said Axel. "I have **beautiful** paws!"

"And he can't **draw**. The art thief is **excellent** at drawing," said Fang.

"OK, I heard cats were **rude**, but this is something else!" complained Axel.

Fang shook her head. "Remember the **terrible drawings** on his desk?"

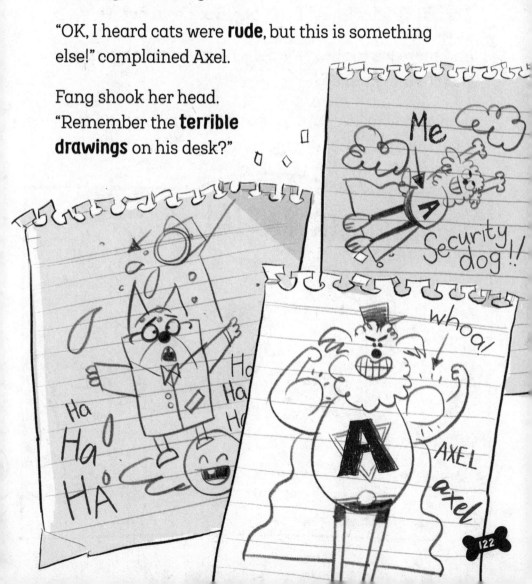

"But how do we explain the **masterpiece** in his office?" said Barkley. But even as he asked the question, he realized he already knew the answer.

"He was **framed**!" said Fang and Barkley together.

And there was only one Woof-O-Bite-chomping dog **clever** enough to do it.

Someone who had **total** access to the gallery and to all of the art. Someone who had lovely **little** paws...

They needed to find him. But he could be anywhere in the gallery. How would they **track** him down?

"We need to get back to your security office and see if we can **spot** Sir Basil on the security TV," said Barkley.

"We don't need to go back to my office to find Sir Basil," said Axel.

Barkley and Fang looked at him, **confused**.

"Why not?" said Barkley.

"Because he's right **there**," said Axel, pointing at Sir Basil.

And, true enough, there he was—**camouflaged** against a painting just outside the bathroom door. He'd heard the whole thing, and he wasn't about to stick around.

"HEY, SIR BASIL!" Axel yelled.
"Did you **lock** me in the toilet?"

AMERIDOG GOTHIC

Sir Basil turned on his paws and ran as fast as his **short** legs could carry him—which was **pretty** fast, actually.

Fang and Barkley set off in hot pursuit.

The Underdogs were faster than Sir Basil—and Fang was a better **climber**—but Sir Basil knew this gallery better than anyone.

He knew all the **shortcuts**, he knew all the **secret passages**—he knew how to stay one step ahead of the Underdogs.

Every time Fang and Barkley got close, Sir Basil **disappeared**.

He **slipped** into the storeroom.

STORE ROOM

He **dashed** through the loading dock.

He **raced** into the workshop where they repaired damaged art.

Fang **slid** along
the tiled hallways.

Barkley **clattered** over
the polished floors.

They **sped** in and out of rooms
filled with art, but Sir Basil
evaded them at **every** turn.

128

The Underdogs raced into a **large** hall. It was filled with marble **statues** of ancient dogs who'd lived centuries ago. All types of dogs, too. **Big** ones, **little** ones, **three-legged** ones.

But where was Sir Basil?

"Here's a corgi," said Barkley, pointing to the statue next to him.

It was a very fancy-looking **corgi** statue... with an **uncanny** resemblance to Sir Basil.

Barkley's eyes opened **wide**.

Just then, the statue **sneezed**.

Sir Basil!

Quick as a **flash**, Barkley grabbed Sir Basil before he could escape again.

Fang gasped. "Barkley, this must be how Sir Basil **swapped** out the paintings. He **camouflaged** himself as a work of art so he wouldn't show up on the **security cameras**!"

"**I CAN EXPLAIN!**" yelped Sir Basil.

"Well?" said Fang.

"I . . ." stammered Sir Basil. "I just like **pretending** to be a statue!"

"Yeah, right," scoffed Barkley.

Sir Basil had turned pale. "Oh, all right! **I CONFESS!** I **swapped** the paintings."

At that moment, Axel entered the hall with Puplo. The artist made a **beeline** for the wriggling corgi. "Axel here has told me you're the **art thief**! Sir Basil, it can't be true!"

Sir Basil nodded glumly. "I'm sorry, Puplo. I didn't mean to **hurt** anyone."

Sir Basil turned to the Underdogs. "Just tell me **ONE THING!** How did you know it was me?" he asked.

Fang smiled.

"First there were the **Woof-O-Bites**. They're your **favorite**, right? Then you found the painting in Axel's office **right away**."

"And when Dr. Spots tested the **fake**, she noticed the canvas was **identical** to the original. How could that be?" asked Barkley.

Because it's the **SAME** canvas! The real masterpiece was on the other side the whole time.

"Come on. Let me **show** you," said Fang.

The Underdogs took Axel, Puplo, and Sir Basil back to the **exhibition**, where Puplo's paintings hung on the wall.

Fang walked over to the fake, took one of her **sharp** claws and **sliced** the back of the painting.

The crowd around her cried out in **horror**. One lemur **tumbled** to the floor in a faint.

"Everyone stay calm," said Barkley. "This is all part of an important **investigation** by us, the Underdogs. If anyone needs a business card, I've got **hundreds**."

Fang pulled away the painting's **cardboard** backing...

... and there on the back of the canvas was the **ORIGINAL MASTERPIECE!**

> My masterpiece! My beautiful masterpiece! Thank you, Underdogs!

"I got the idea when I saw Sir Basil search Axel's office for clues. Remember how he **flipped** the bulletin board around? That's how he had hidden the original artwork in plain sight."

"It was a **genius** hiding place! By a genius **artist**!" Sir Basil squealed.

"Is that why you did it?" asked Fang. "To prove to the world that you are as **good** an artist as Puplo Picasso?"

The crowd pressed closer, looking **expectantly** at Sir Basil.

"I just wanted people to see my paintings!" cried Sir Basil. "I **love** to paint, and people only think of me as a stuffy old corgi. I'm an **artist** too, you know!"

Fang turned to the crowd. "He swapped out the **original** painting for the **fake** he had created," she explained. "He was hoping he could **fool** everybody who saw it, but he didn't fool Puplo."

Barkley grinned.

And he didn't fool the Underdogs either.

"Oh, and there's **one** more thing that gave you away..." added Barkley.

"What's that?" sniffed Sir Basil.

"You hired **us**," said Barkley. "You thought we wouldn't be able to crack the case, but you **underestimated** us."

Sir Basil sighed. "I certainly did. I never thought you'd catch me!"

Fang and Barkley **smiled** at each other.

Suddenly, Axel piped up. "Hey, let's not forget that to get people off his scent, Sir Basil **framed** me by hiding a **stolen** artwork in my office!"

Sir Basil looked at the ground. He'd done the **wrong** thing, and he knew it. "I'm **sorry**. I truly am. How will I **ever** make it up to everyone?"

You can start by giving me a promotion!

Done!

"And I want a **bag** of **bones**!" added Axel.

Fang smiled. "That's a good **start**, but it's not just Axel you need to make it up to…"

After the Underdogs had **cracked** the **case**, a few things happened.

Sir Basil decided it was time to make the gallery a whole lot less **snooty**, and even let in some **new** artists, like this one ...

And **this** one ...

SOUP

A life
in soup.

Carl

But even that wasn't enough to make up for all the
trouble Sir Basil had caused with a paintbrush.

So Sir Basil decided to set things **right** ... and it turns
out he was pretty **handy**!

After a coat of paint, the Underdogs' agency was looking **better** than **new**.

And because Sir Basil was feeling **particularly** bad about what he'd done, he painted the Underdogs something **extra special** on the ceiling.

"Not bad, Basil!" said Fang.

Sir Basil beamed with **pride**. "Yes, after all this I may have finally found my true calling. I'm going into business as a **painter**."

Barkley and Dr. Spots nodded. The detective agency looked a **whole** lot better now.

"That's a **great** idea!" added Carl. "Say, do you have any paint left over? There's just a little something that needs touching up…"

Carl snapped up the **paintbrush** and **bucket** (after all, he was an artist!) and climbed the fire escape to the very top of their building.

"I think it needs a little **something**…" said Carl, as he worked his **magic** with the paint.

DO **YOU** HAVE WHAT IT TAKES TO BE AN **UNDERDOG** DETECTIVE?

SEARCH & FIND

A good detective can find hidden evidence. Can you find these ten words in the below grid?

**DALMATIAN   CASE   DELIVERY   PHONE   SNEAKY
FAMOUS   PAINTING   IMITATION   PAW   CLUES**

K X Y Z X Y G Y S B O O H G W
E R F T A S G O D U N Y B P G
I R P F C T Y P P O O Q W S G
Z Z F Y Y U L W I C W M B I N
V W B W M X C T R G A Z A P I
K F D A L M A T I A N S H F T
D A M J N T F R L W J O E O N
E D C P I M Q E Z U N P U I I
L J J M I N B T Z E W Y L Y A
I Z I X B R Y V A P A W H S P
V O A C K L I S C V Q Q Z A G
E F F M L V T H X I A Y A P W
R Y E Q G U S H W C H J J I E
Y K A E N S E G R E B T F S T
O L S M L D F S O Z H Q D Y K

WORD SCRAMBLE

A good detective uses clues to solve a mystery. Can you complete the below sentence by unscrambling the ten clues?

If the Underdogs weren't so good with their disguises, solving these mysteries might be _ _ _ _ _ _ _ _ _ _ _ _ !

RVEIHSED	_ _ O _ _ _ _ _
AREPESTCEMI	O _ _ _ _ _ _ _ _ _
IRSEPPDEDAA	_ _ _ _ O _ _ _ _ _
CFRYOAT	_ O _ _ _ _ _
ONDOGWT	_ _ _ _ _ O _
ETIADRSS	_ _ O _ O _ _ _ _
GNSAETIL	_ _ _ _ _ O _ _
BDRAKE	O _ _ _ _ _
RLLYEGA	_ _ _ O _ _ _
ODAENPT	_ _ _ O _ _ _

A good detective knows when something is out of place. Can you find the ten differences between these two pictures?

:paw: ANSWER KEY :paw:

So how did you do?

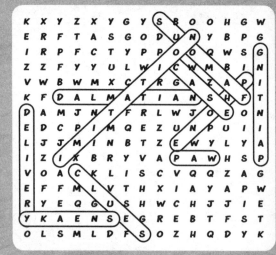

WORD SCRAMBLE

Shivered, Masterpiece,
Disappeared, Factory,
Dogtown, Disaster,
Stealing, Barked,
Gallery, Notepad

Answer to the clues:
im*paw*ssible!

SPOT THE DIFFERENCE

*If you speak to Carl, hang up and call back until someone else answers.

COMING SOON
Puplo
OFF THE LEASH
AN EXHIBITION OF
PUPLO PICASSO'S
GREATEST WORKS
ONLY AT
DOGTOWN ART GALLERY

CRIME IS ON THE RISE IN DOGTOWN, AND IT'S ALL THANKS TO A DOGGONE THIEF!

It's nearly time for the Dogtown Tennis Grand Slam, but all the balls have mysteriously gone missing. Could Boris Barker, the famed international tennis pro, be behind it all? Or what about Steffi Gruff? Or Novak Dogavic? No matter who the culprit is, if they're not stopped, the tournament will be ruined. . .

So it's time to call in the Underdog Detective Agency! And they jump on the case like a dog with a ball, but can they save the day and serve up the criminal mastermind in time? Or will it be game, set, match?